D0251529

ALLIGATORS
ALL AROUND
AN ALPHABET

ALLIGATORS
ALL AROUND

by
MAURICE SENDAK

AN ALPHABET

HarperCollins*Publishers*

ALLIGATORS ALL AROUND
Copyright © 1962 by Maurice Sendak
Copyright renewed 1990 by Maurice Sendak
Manufactured in China.
All rights reserved.
For information address HarperCollins Children's Books,
a division of HarperCollins Publishers,
195 Broadway, New York, NY 10007.
Library of Congress catalog card number: 62-13315
ISBN 0-06-025530-7 (lib. bdg.)
17 18 19 20 SCP 20 19 18 17 16 15 14

 alligators all around

 bursting balloons

C catching colds

D doing dishes

E entertaining elephants

F forever fooling

G getting giggles

 having headaches

 imitating Indians

J

juggling jelly beans

 keeping kangaroos

L

looking like lions

M making macaroni

N never napping

 ordering oatmeal

P

pushing people

 quite quarrelsome

 riding reindeer

S

shockingly spoiled

T throwing tantrums

U

usually upside down

V very vain

W

wearing wigs

X

x-ing x's

Y yackety-yacking

Z

Zippity zound!
Alligators ALL around.